TRACE YOUR HAND &
DRAW
· FARM ANIMALS ·

MAÏTÉ BALART

TABLE OF CONTENTS

HERE ARE ALL THE ANIMALS AND CHARACTERS YOU WILL FIND IN THIS BOOK!

Quarto is the authority on a wide range of topics.
Quarto educates, entertains, and enriches the lives of our readers—
enthusiasts and lovers of hands-on living.
www.quartoknows.com

© 2016 Quarto Publishing Group USA Inc.
Published by Walter Foster Publishing,
a division of Quarto Publishing Group USA Inc.
All rights reserved. Walter Foster is a registered trademark.

Translated by Marion Serre.

The original French edition was published as *Animaux de la ferme*.
© 2014, Mila Éditions – 2ter rue des Chantiers, 75005 Paris

6 Orchard Road, Suite 100
Lake Forest, CA 92630
quartoknows.com
Visit our blogs at quartoknows.com

MIX
Paper from
responsible sources
FSC® C101537

Printed in China
1 3 5 7 9 10 8 6 4 2

TOOLS & MATERIALS

ALL YOU NEED IS YOUR HAND AND A PENCIL OR CRAYON TO GET STARTED.

FOLLOW THE SIMPLE STEPS TO CREATE EACH FARM ANIMAL,
AND THEN DRAW A FUN SCENE AROUND THEM.

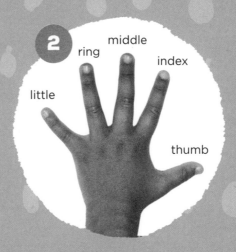

You will need crayons or
pencils and your hand!

Look at the names
of each of your fingers.

COW

1

2

3

4

KATIE THE COW LOVES TO EAT GRASS.

GOOSE

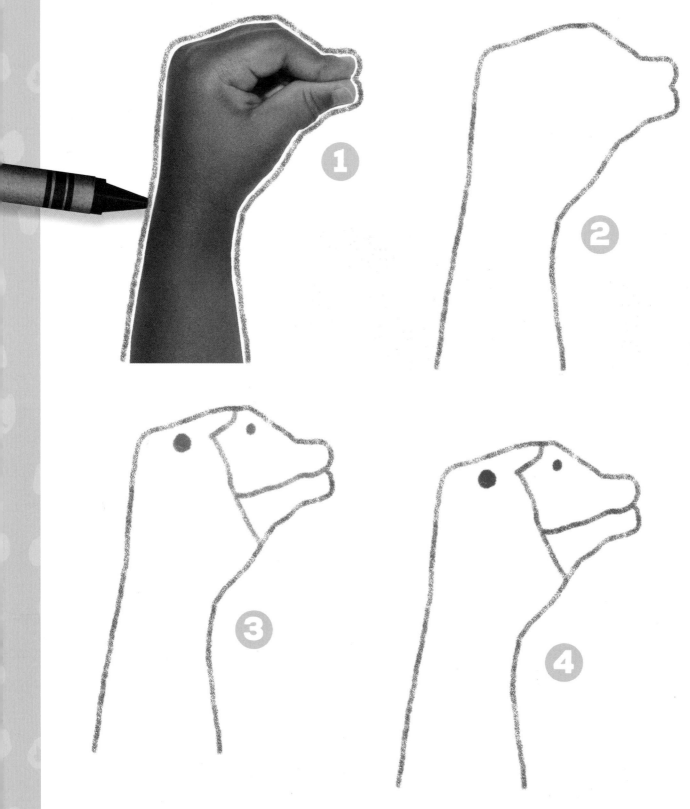

GRETA AND GLORIA, TWO GEESE, HONK LOUDLY WITH THEIR BEAUTIFUL VOICES.

RABBIT

ROGER AND RUBY THE RABBITS ENJOY
A LITTLE STROLL IN THE GARDEN.

HORSE

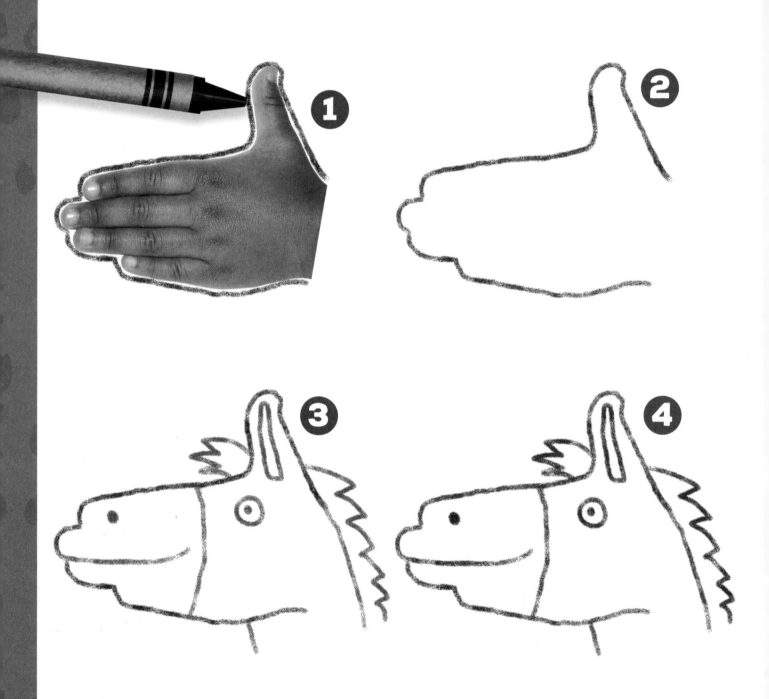

THE HORSES LOOK BEAUTIFUL AS
THEY GALLOP AWAY.

ROOSTER

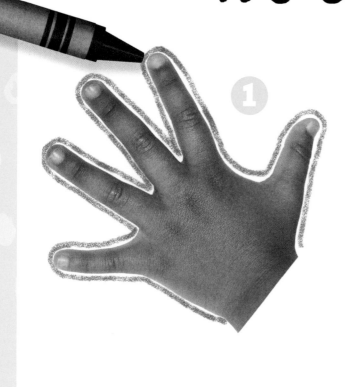

REGINALD THE ROOSTER IS THE KING OF THE BARNYARD.

CHICKS

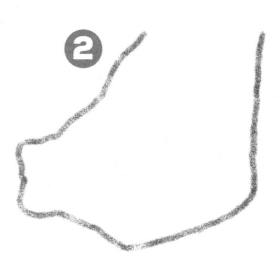

THE LITTLE CHICKS, MILLY, TILLY, AND DILLY,
STICK TOGETHER AS THEY LOOK FOR GRAIN.

FARMER'S WIFE

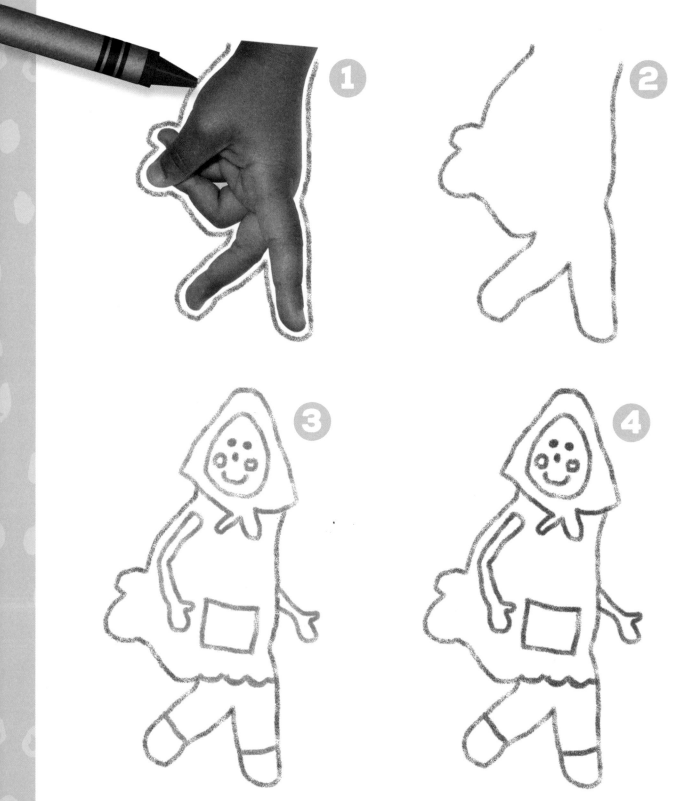

BEATRICE, THE FARMER'S WIFE, THROWS GRAIN ON THE GROUND FOR THE CHICKENS.

PIG

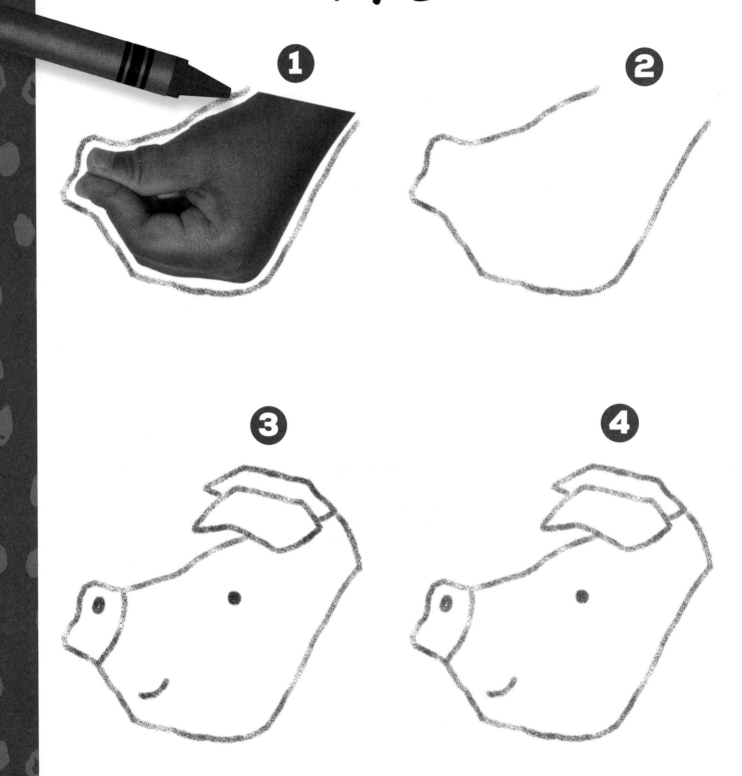

FROG

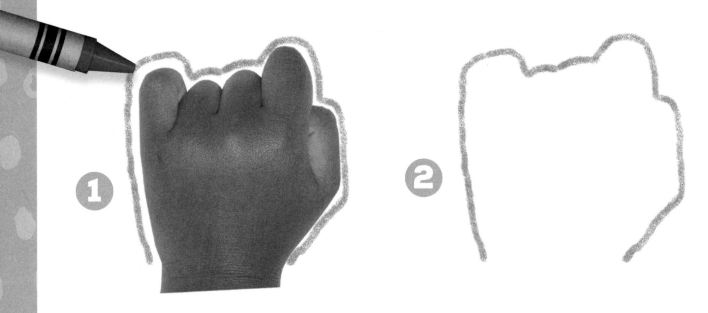

1

2

3

4

PERCHED ON THE WATER LILIES, THE
FROGS ADMIRE THE POND.

SWAN

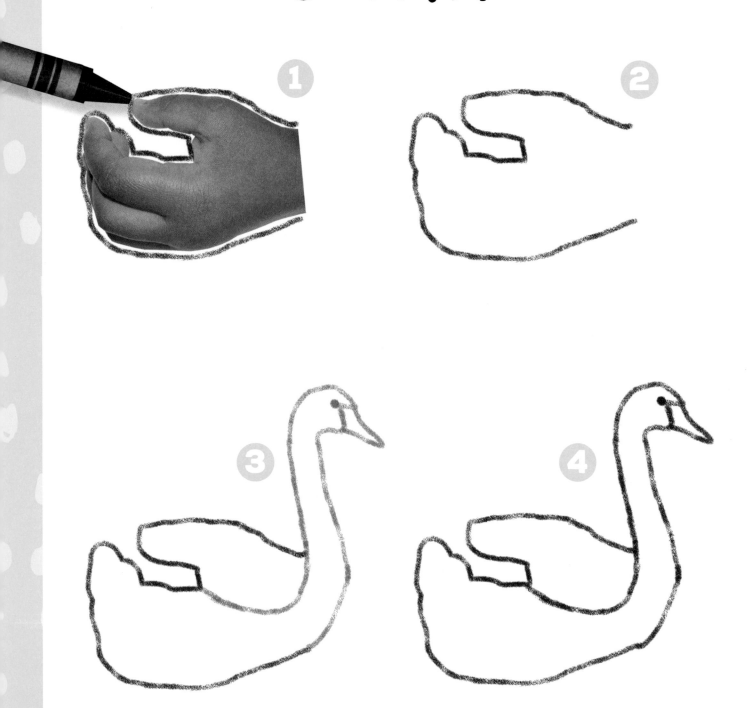

SEBASTIAN THE SWAN MAJESTICALLY
SWIMS ACROSS THE POND.

BEEKEEPER

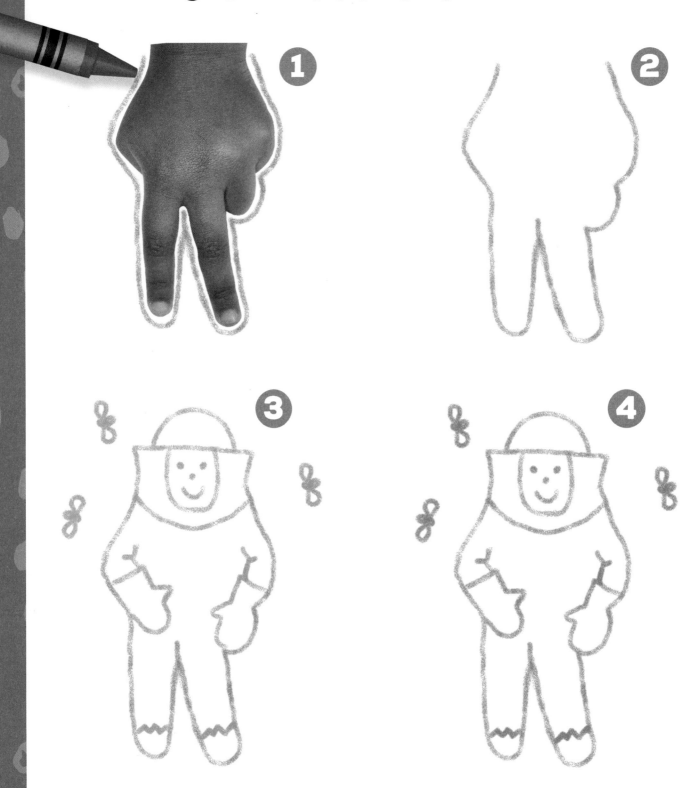

BERTIE, THE BRAVE BEEKEEPER, COLLECTS
HONEY FROM THE BEEHIVES.

BEES

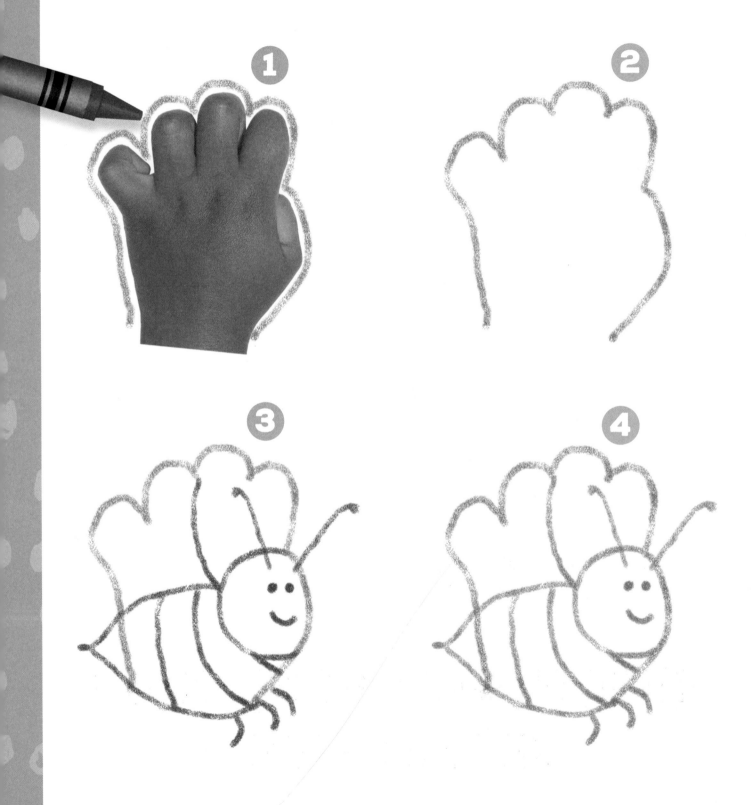

THE BEES BUZZ HAPPILY, COLLECTING POLLEN TO MAKE HONEY.

APPLE TREE

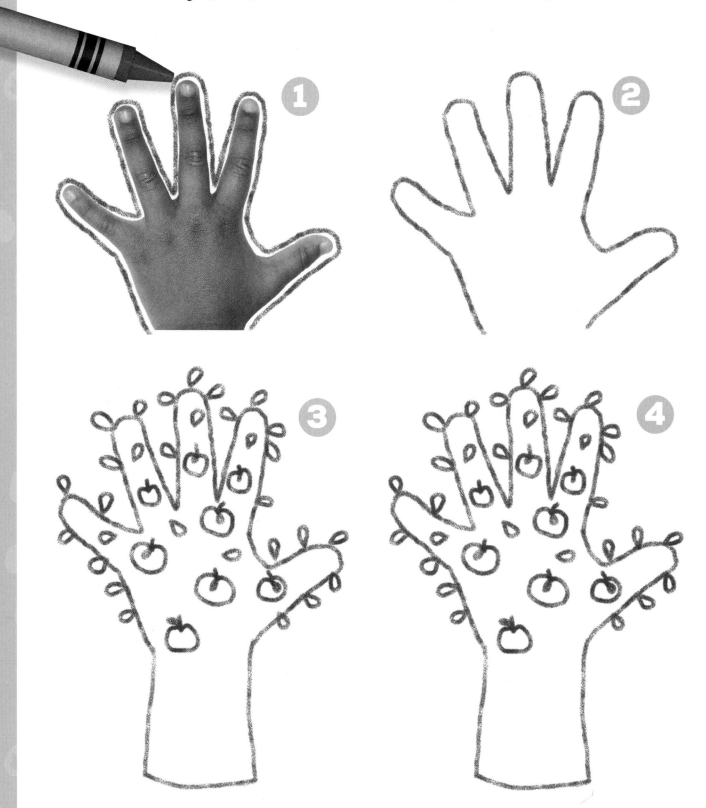

DELICIOUS, CRUNCHY APPLES HAVE FALLEN
FROM THE TREE IN THE ORCHARD.
LET'S GO PICK THEM UP!

FARMHOUSE

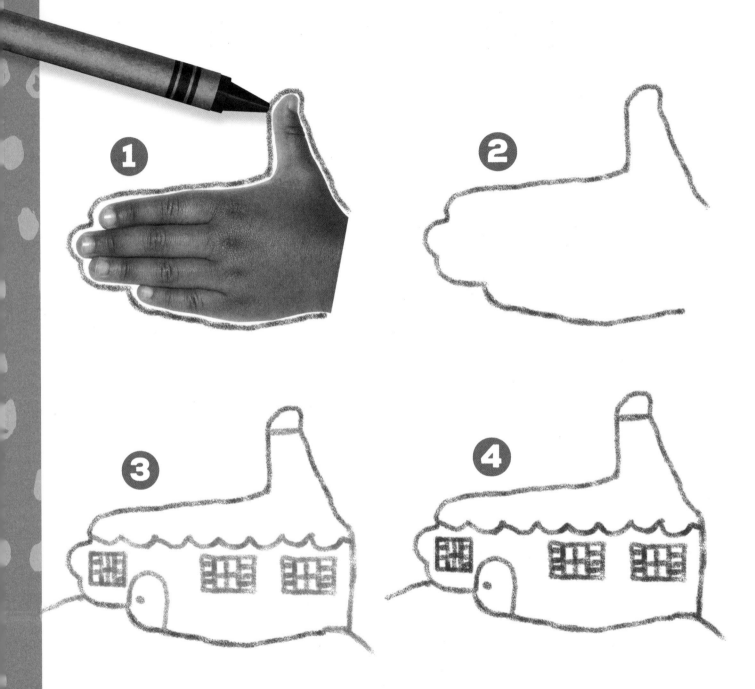

THE FARMHOUSE IS JUST AT
THE END OF THE ROAD.

GOAT

THE YOUNG GOATS, MOLLY, POLLY, AND DOLLY, NEVER STOP EATING.

OWL

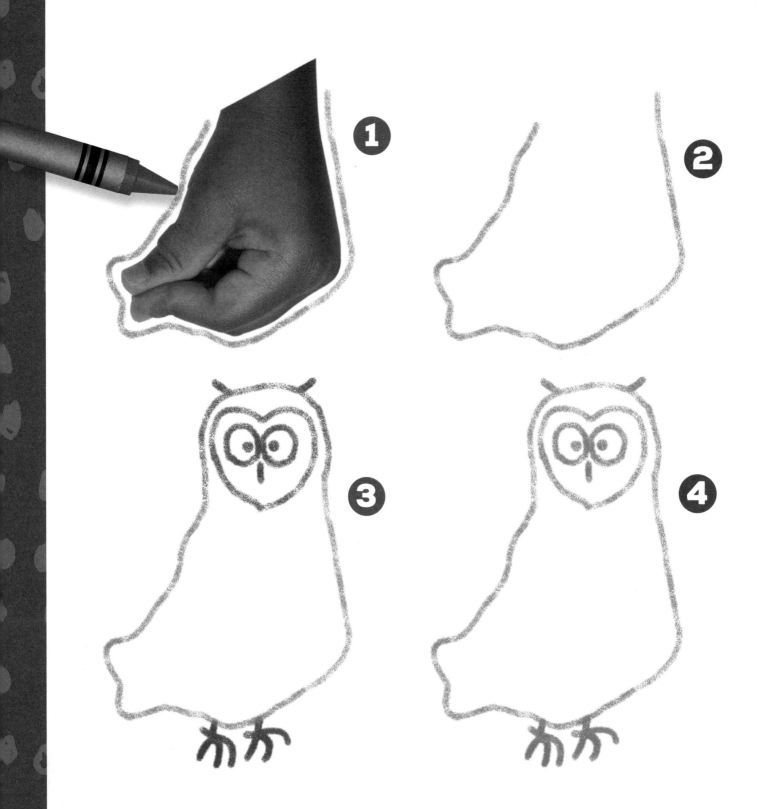

OSCAR THE OWL HOOTS AT DUSK.

SHEEP

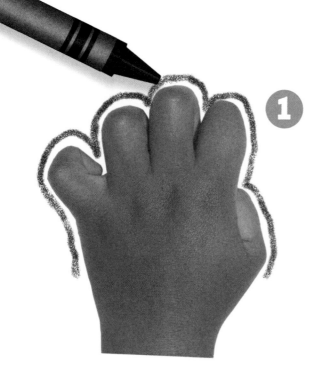

DUCK

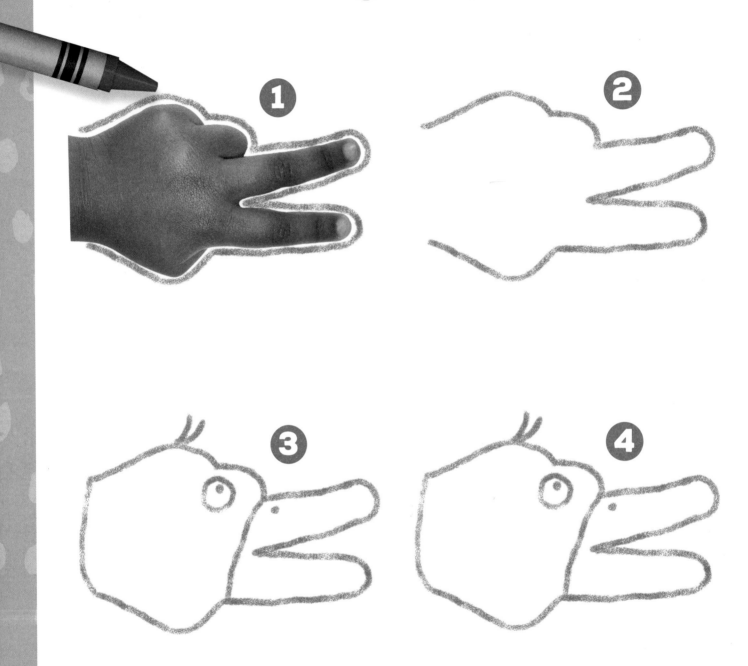

DEREK THE DUCK SPLASHES IN THE POND.

DOG

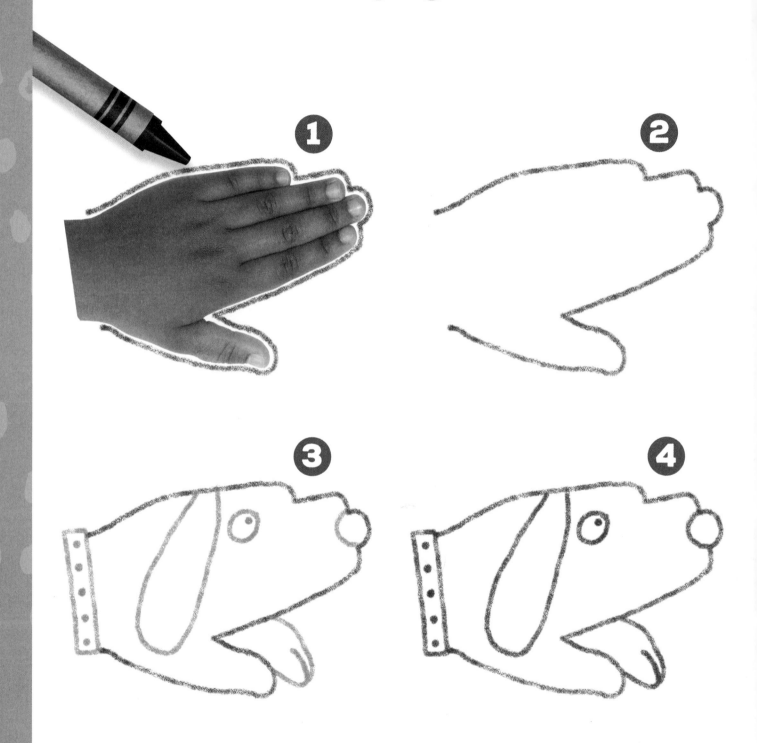

HIS BOWL IS EMPTY,
BUT DOUG THE DOG
IS STILL HUNGRY!

TURKEY

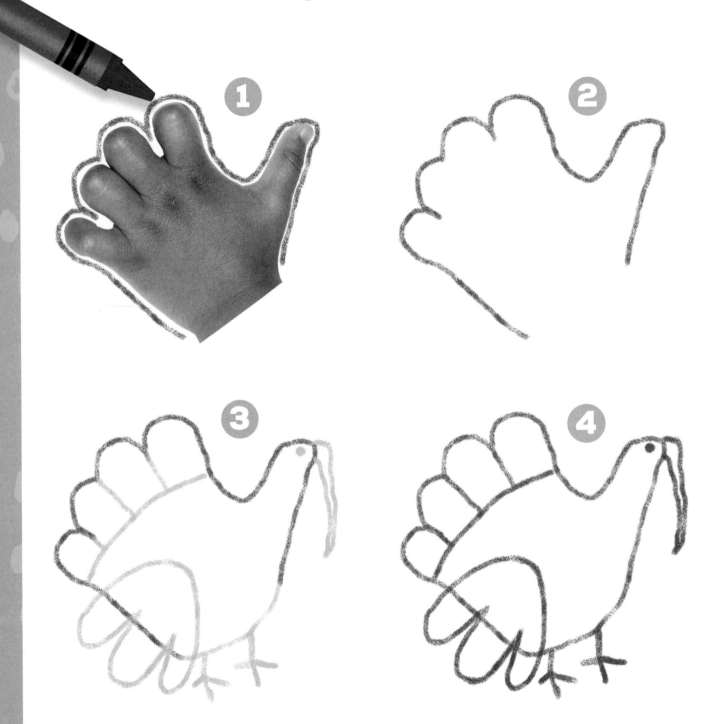

TOMMY THE TURKEY GOBBLE-GOBBLES
NEAR THE FENCE.

TRACTOR

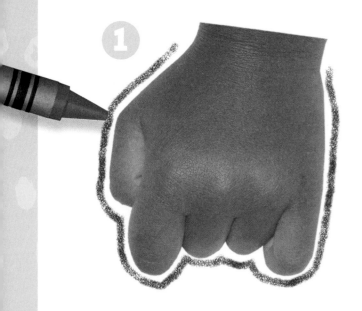

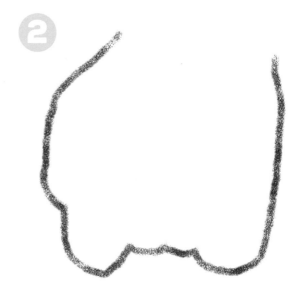

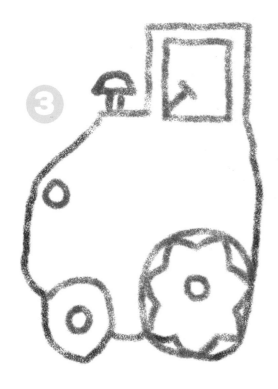

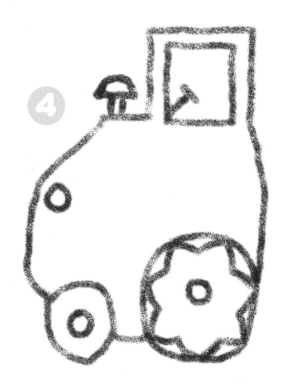

THE LITTLE TRACTOR WORKS IN THE FIELDS.

MOUSE

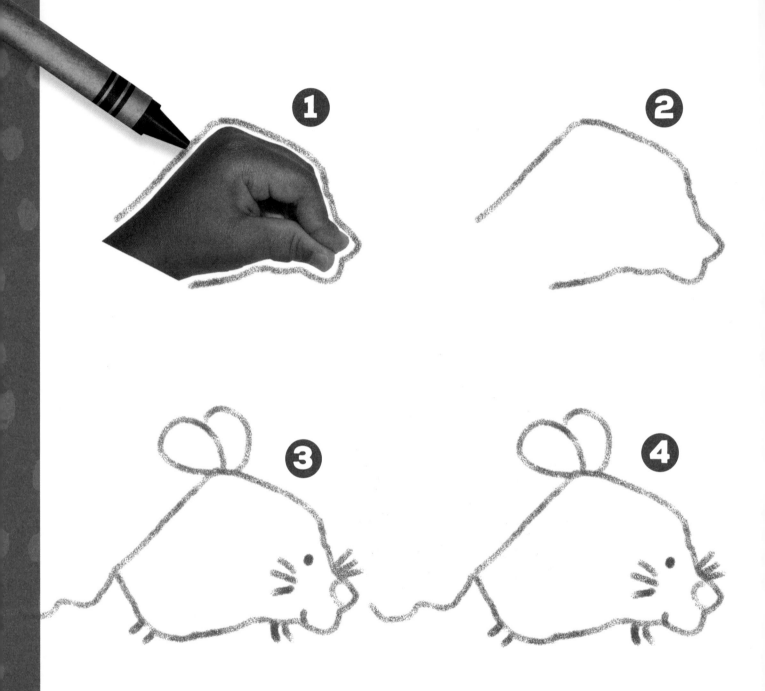

FREDDY THE FIELD MOUSE DASHES THROUGH THE HAY FIELDS.

WHAT OTHER ANIMALS CAN YOU MAKE
WITH YOUR HAND?

CREATE A FUN FARM SCENE WITH
ALL OF THE ANIMALS YOU HAVE NOW
LEARNED TO DRAW!